Brian Wildsmith

The Apple Bird

Oxford University Press

Oxford Toronto Melbourne

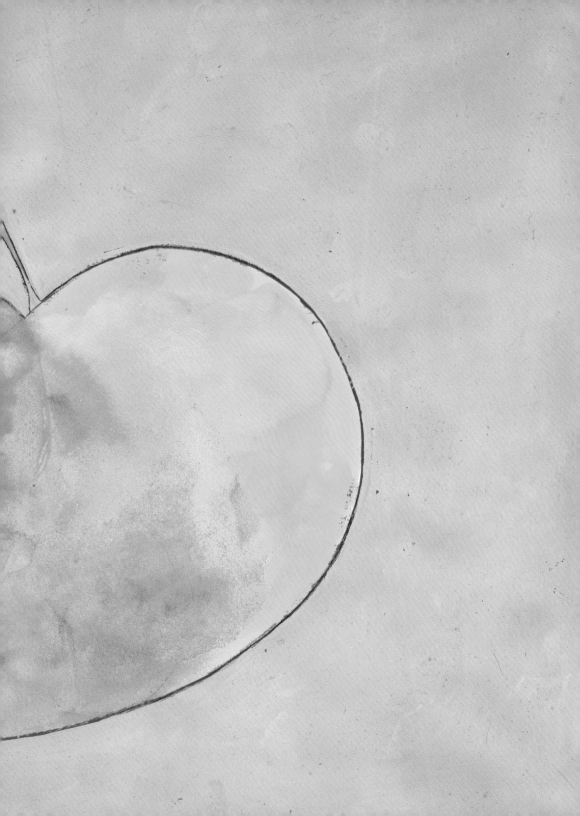

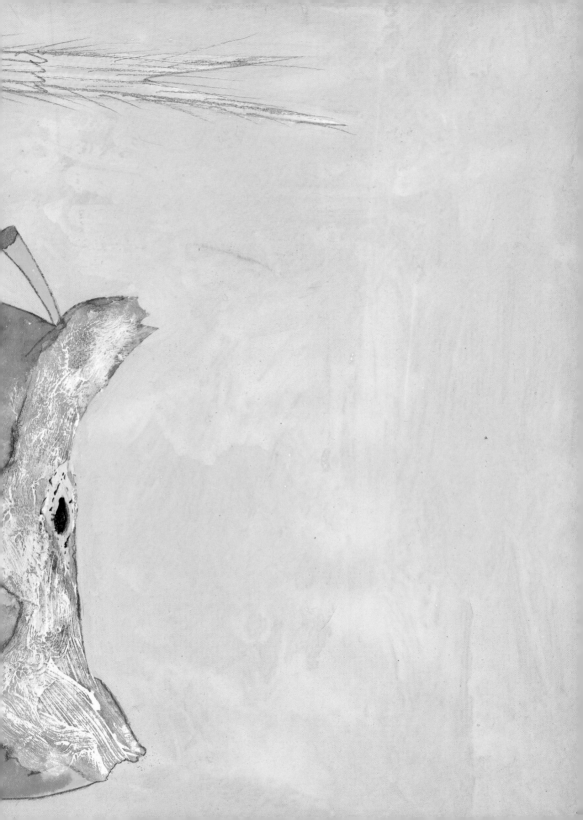

Oxford University Press, Walton Street, Oxford OX2 6DP

Oxford New York Toronto
Delhi Bombay Calcutta Madras Karachi
Petaling Jaya Singapore Hong Kong Tokyo
Nairobi Dar es Salaam Cape Town
Melbourne Auckland
and associated companies in
Berlin Ibadan
Oxford is a trade mark of Oxford University Press

© Brian Wildsmith 1983
First published 1983
Reprinted 1984 (twice), 1985, 1986, 1989 (twice)

British Library Cataloguing in Publication Data
Wildsmith, Brian
The apple bird.
I. Title
823'.914[J] PZ7
ISBN 0-19-272136-4

Printed in Hong Kong

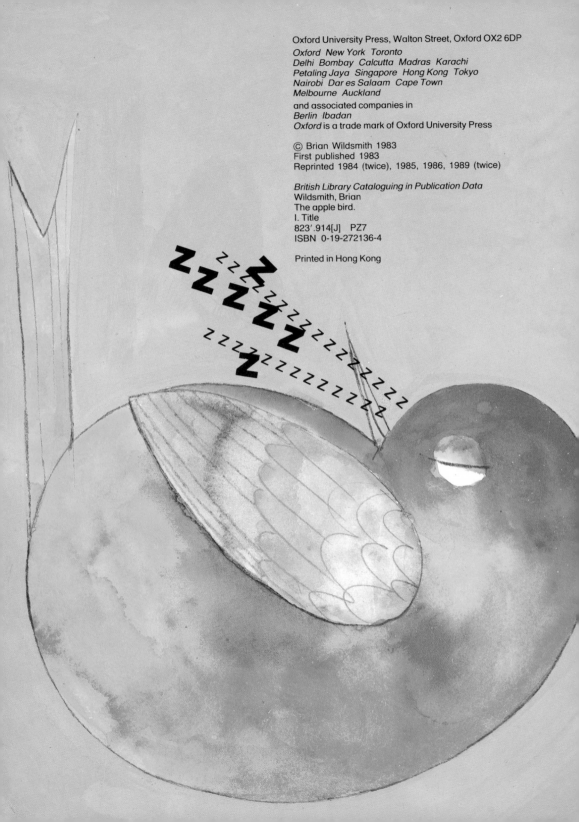